BVL

W9-BVZ-067

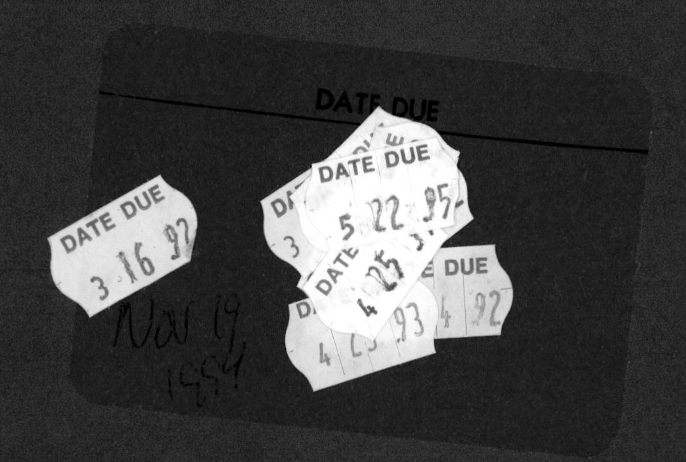
DATE DUE
DATE DUE
3 16 92
DATE DUE
5 22 95
E DUE
4 92
93

A NOTE ABOUT THE STORY

Warren Ludwig has enjoyed reading the Bible and drawing pictures since he was a young boy. But it wasn't until recently, when he was reading up on elephant legends, that Warren found the opportunity to bring the two together. He came across an Israeli folktale that told of a "dangerous situation" on the ark, and it piqued his interest. Here was a chance to renew his acquaintance with Noah—in Warren's words, "an old friend from my childhood"—and to add his own comic sensibility to ark lore without altering the biblical flood story.

The result is a warmly personal "what if" account of life on Noah's ark, sparkling with the author's sense of humor and visual wit. This is the first Whitebird Book to draw on the beloved personalities and situations of the Bible, and we're proud to have a person of Warren Ludwig's faith and talent to do it.

—Tomie dePaola, Creative Director
WHITEBIRD BOOKS

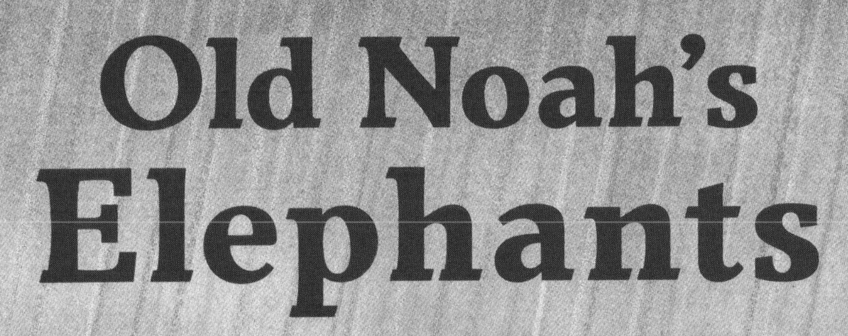

An Israeli folktale adapted and illustrated by

Warren Ludwig

A WHITEBIRD BOOK
G.P. Putnam's Sons
New York

To Courtney, Mom, and Dad,
with all my love.

Thanks also to Rabbi Lawrence Pinsker
for his research into the name of Noah's wife.

G.P. Putnam's Sons, a division of The Putnam & Grosset Book Group,
200 Madison Avenue, New York, NY 10016.
Published simultaneously in Canada.
Printed in Hong Kong by South China Printing Co. (1988) Ltd.
Book design by Gunta Alexander
Library of Congress Cataloging-in-Publication Data.
Ludwig, Warren. Old Noah's elephants : an Israeli folktale / retold and
illustrated by Warren Ludwig. p. c.m. "A Whitebird book."
Summary: When the misbehavior of the two elephants aboard Noah's
ark threatens the survival of the other animals, God tells Noah that
the solution is to tickle the hyena.
[1. Noah (Biblical figure)—Folklore. 2. Noah's ark—Folklore.
3. Folklore—Israel.] I. Title. PZ8.1.L96801 1991
398.22'095694—dc20 [E] 90-35379 CIP AC
ISBN 0-399-22256-1
10 9 8 7 6 5 4 3 2 1
First Impression

"So there you are!" said Noah's wife, Emzara, as she hurried outside. "Noah, I think you should come and see what your elephants are doing."

"What now?" Noah sighed. It was hard enough just
keeping the ark in one piece. Between feeding the animals

and soothing ruffled feathers, Noah's family was busy all the time. There was always something that needed attention.

"Just look at those two," Emzara said. "Last night, when everyone was sleeping, they wandered in here and found the food supplies."

"If you don't do something, they'll eat everything in sight," she warned. "You tell them we already *have* two pigs."

"Don't worry, dear wife," Noah said. "I'll take care of it."

"All right, Mr. and Mrs. Elephant," Noah said. "Please go back to your room. You must wait until feeding time like all the other animals."

The elephants just smiled and kept eating.
"I said, it's time to go back to your room…now."

But the elephants still wouldn't move.
"Enough of this nonsense," Noah said, and he pushed on them with all of his might.

Yet the harder he pushed, the faster they ate. And the faster they ate, the fatter they became.

Noah soon grew tired and sat down to think. After a while, he noticed something strange was happening.

"Oh, my!" Noah cried. "Those elephants are so fat the ark is tipping over!"

Noah began praying. "What should I do, God? We'll all perish if I can't get the elephants to move."

"Tickle the hyena," replied the Lord.
"What?" Noah asked, quite surprised.
"Tickle the hyena," the Lord said again. "Trust me."

So who was Noah to argue? He found a goose feather
and tickled a hyena on the nose.

The hyena screamed with laughter and nearly rolled on top of the lion's tail.
"*Roar!*" growled the lion.

All of the noise made a giraffe jump. His head bumped a monkey asleep on the rafters.

The monkey fell onto a zebra's back. The zebra kicked and kicked. *Splash!* Over went a barrel full of fish.

A moose stepped on one of the slippery wet fish and slid across the floor. *Thud!* Right into a hippo.

The hippo sat down and almost flattened two chickens and a peacock.
"*Squawk!*"

"Yap! Yap! Yap!" barked a dog, and it began to chase the chickens.

When the dog ran by, it scared a cat, who leaped over a rhino and surprised a mouse.

The mouse hurried into a basket of vegetables and hid under a big green cabbage.

Suddenly...the big green cabbage disappeared!

"Squeak."

The elephants were terrified! They dropped what they were eating and ran off to opposite ends of the ark.

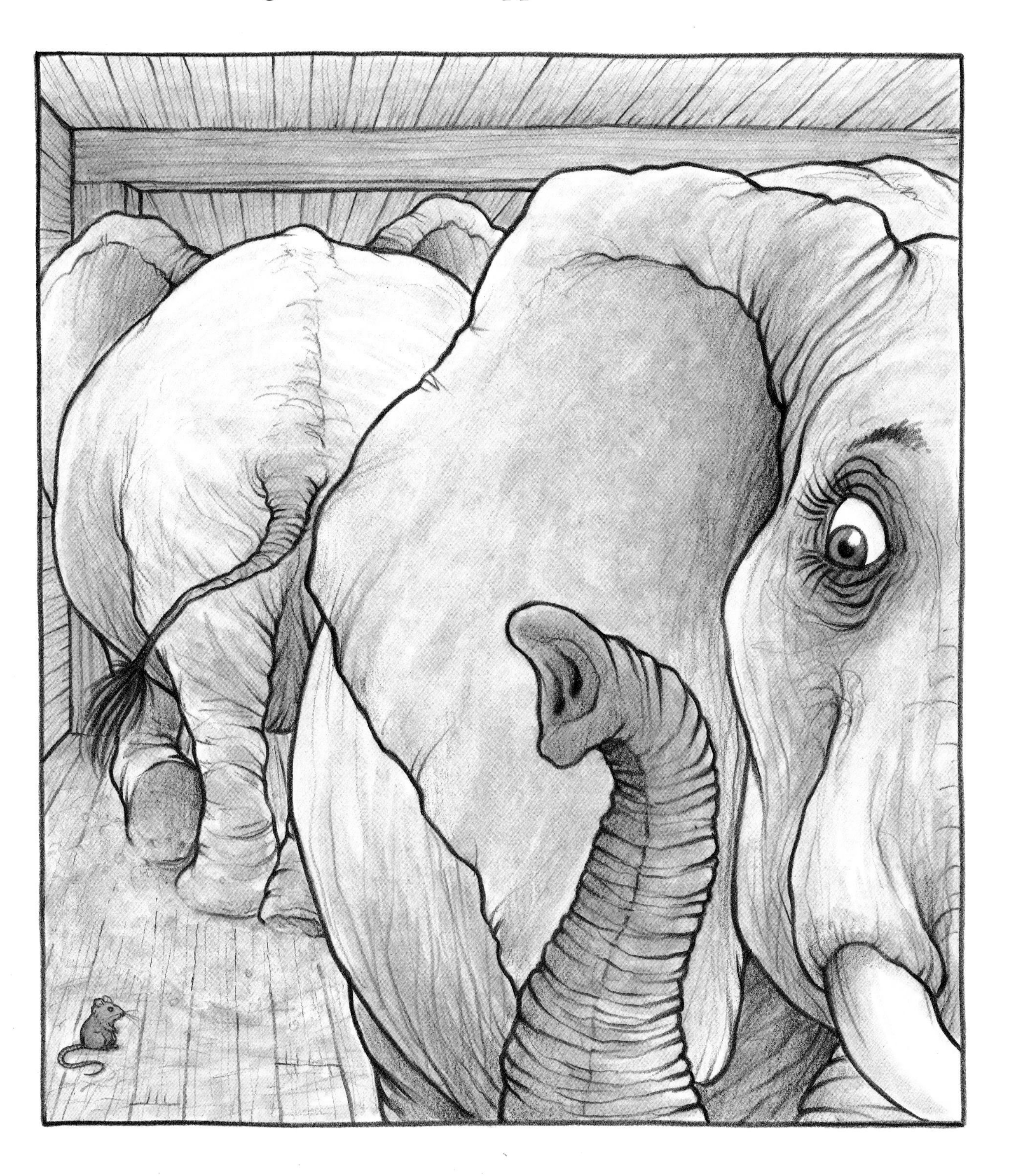

“We’re saved!” Noah cheered. “We’re saved!”
That evening, Noah and his family thanked God

for answering Noah's prayer. They held a big celebration that lasted long into the night.

“Have you seen the termites today?” Emzara asked.
“I can’t find them anywhere.”
Noah’s eyes were closing. “We’ll look for them tomorrow,”
he said. And he kissed his wife good night.